To Nigel

Text and illustrations copyright © 1981 by Jenny Partridge
Published by World's Work Ltd
The Windmill Press, Kingswood, Tadworth, Surrey
Layout and design by The Romany Studio Workshop
Reproduced by Graphic Affairs Ltd, Southend
Printed in Great Britain by
William Clowes (Beccles) Limited, Beccles and London
Second impression 1982
SBN 437 66175 X

Dominic Sly

JENNY PARTRIDGE

A WORLD'S WORK CHILDREN'S BOOK

Dominic Sly picked up his fiddle
and began to play another jolly tune.
His collecting cap was still empty
and so was his poor stomach!

Surely someone in Oakapple Wood liked his
music – but one or two woodlanders actually
frowned at him and remarked how peaceful
the wood had been before his arrival!

He was soon interrupted
by the gruff voice of Sergeant Quilp.
"Come on now, move along please."
"But officer," pleaded Dominic,
"I am only trying to make an honest
penny to buy my supper!"

"Well go and do it elsewhere,"
said Quilp sternly. "Folks around here
like a bit of peace and quiet. Off with you
and take that wretched fiddle with you!"

Dominic sadly packed his things
and was about to pick up his empty cap

when Colonel Grunt and his old friend
Major Snout approached him.

"By Jove," said Snout, "what a jolly tune
– why I haven't heard a fiddle for years."
He threw two pennies into Dominic's cap.
"Thank you sir," Dominic grinned broadly.
"Come along, Snout,"
muttered Colonel Grunt irritably.
"We're wasting time with this ragamuffin!"

As they hurried off,
a loud crack of thunder
echoed around the wood
and it started to rain.

Dominic gathered up the two pennies
and made his way to Pollensnuff Stores,
where he bought himself a large slice of
Mrs Pollensnuff's hawthorn and
raspberry pie for his supper.

He scurried to Bramble Copse
and made himself cosy amid the primroses
in the shelter of an old tree root.
All around him the rain fell in large drops
and the thunder crashed, as he ate
his supper hungrily.

"My, that was good."
He wiped the last crumb from his whiskers
and settled down for a snooze.

While Dominic snored softly under his tree,
the rain gradually ceased
and night fell upon the wood.

He was awoken early next morning
by gossiping voices.
"Well, they do say he's quite poorly,"

Grandma Snuffles was saying.
"Must have been caught in that dreadful
storm last night," replied Mrs Twitcher.
"Poor old soul!"

"Morning ladies!" said Dominic,
brushing himself down.
"Can I play you a tune for my breakfast?"

"Certainly not!"
said Mrs Twitcher sternly.
"How can you think about such things
when that nice Major Snout is lying ill
with a bad chill on his chest up
at Mayfly Manor?"

"What's that you say?" asked Dominic.
"Why I only saw him yesterday
and he was in fine spirits!
Poor old chap – perhaps I can help."
"Huh, how could a scalliwag
like you help?" snapped Mrs Twitcher.

Now, Dominic had been a travelling musician for many years, and knew the hedgerow well.

He had a remedy for everything,
from snake bite to a cold in the head!
He gathered several herbs and plants from
nearby bushes and set off for Mayfly Manor.

Colonel Grunt was most annoyed to see
Dominic again, but Clara the cook
persuaded him to try out the 'hedgerow cure'.

Once inside, Dominic told Clara exactly
how to prepare the mixture of leaves, and
soon it was bubbling away on the stove.
"Pah!" muttered the Colonel.

Upstairs in the guest room poor Major Snout was feeling very ill indeed. He was quite weak from sneezing and wondered if he would ever be his old self again.

Clara came in carrying a steaming bowl.
Major Snout wrinkled his nose.
"I'd rather have a tot of blackcurrant rum,"
he said miserably.

He took a sip of the potion.
Ugh! it tasted awful,
but as he drank,
the room seemed to fill
with the merry notes
of Dominic's fiddle.

The more he drank
the louder the music seemed to be,
until at last he had finished every drop!

"By Jove, I feel better already!"
he declared, banging his spoon in time
to the music. He jumped out of bed
and actually danced a jig
before anyone could stop him!

Colonel Grunt looked on in astonishment,
but even he couldn't help
tapping his foot to the music!

"Now don't overdo it," Clara told Major Snout as she helped him back to bed.
A bottle of blackcurrant rum was opened

and they all drank a toast to Dominic,
the travelling musician, and his magic cure –
even Colonel Grunt!